THE HAUNTED BOOKSHELF

The telling or reading of ghost stories during long, dark, and cold Christmas nights is a yuletide ritual dating back to at least the eighteenth century, and was once as much a part of Christmas tradition as decorating fir trees, feasting on goose, and the singing of carols. During the Victorian era many magazines printed ghost stories specifically for the Christmas season. These "winter tales" didn't necessarily explore Christmas themes. Rather, they were offered as an eerie pleasure to be enjoyed on Christmas Eve with the family, adding a supernatural shiver to the seasonal chill.

The tradition remained strong in the British Isles (and her colonies) throughout much of the twentieth century, though in recent years it has been on the wane. Certainly, few people in Canada or the United States seem to know about it any longer. This series of small books seeks to rectify this, to revive a charming custom for the long, dark nights we all know so well here at Christmastime.

THE HAUNTED BOOKSHELF

Charles Dickens
The Signalman

A.M. Burrage
One Who Saw

Edith Wharton
Afterward

M.R. James
The Diary of Mr. Poynter

Marjorie Bowen
The Crown Derby Plate

E.F. Benson
How Fear Departed the Long Gallery

W.W. Jacobs
The Toll House

Algernon Blackwood
The Empty House

H. Russell Wakefield
The Red Lodge

Frank Cowper
Christmas Eve on a Haunted Hulk

R.H. Malden
The Sundial

Elizabeth Gaskell
The Old Nurse's Story

Daphne du Maurier
The Apple Tree

Richard Bridgeman
The Morgan Trust

M.R. James
The Story of a Disappearance and an Appearance

Walter de la Mare
The Green Room

Margaret Oliphant
The Open Door

THE HAUNTED BOOKSHELF

Bernard Capes
An Eddy on the Floor

F. Marion Crawford
The Doll's Ghost

Edith Wharton
Mr. Jones

Shirley Jackson
A Visit

Cynthia Asquith
The Corner Shop

Gertrude Atherton
The Dead and the Countess

Arthur Conan Doyle
The Captain of the Polestar

Marjorie Bowen
The House by the Poppy Field

Andrew Caldecott
A Room in a Rectory

L.P. Hartley
Podolo

Laurence Whistler
Captain Dalgety Returns

Mary Fitt
The Amethyst Cross

Rosemary Timperley
The Mistress in Black

Sarah Orne Jewett
Lady Ferry

H. Russell Wakefield
Lucky's Grove

Edith Wharton
The Duchess at Prayer

Hugh Walpole
The Little Ghost

Louisa Baldwin
The Weird of the Walfords

THE DUCHESS AT PRAYER

The DUCHESS at PRAYER

EDITH WHARTON

A GHOST STORY FOR CHRISTMAS

DESIGNED & DECORATED BY SETH

BIBLIOASIS

I

HAVE YOU EVER questioned the long-shuttered front of an old Italian house, that motionless mask, smooth, mute, equivocal as the face of a priest behind which buzz the secrets of the confessional? Other houses declare the activities they shelter; they are the clear expressive cuticle of a life flowing close to the surface; but the old palace in its narrow street, the villa on its cypress-hooded hill, are as impenetrable as death. The tall windows are like blind eyes, the great door is a shut mouth. Inside there may be sunshine, the scent of myrtles, and a pulse of life through all the arteries of the huge frame; or a mortal solitude where bats lodge in the disjointed stones, and the keys rust in unused doors…

II

FROM THE LOGGIA, with its vanishing frescoes, I looked down an avenue barred by a ladder of cypress shadows to the ducal escutcheon and mutilated vases of the gate. Flat noon lay on the gardens, on fountains, porticoes, and grottoes. Below the terrace, where a chrome-coloured lichen had sheeted the balustrade as with fine laminæ of gold, vineyards stooped to the rich valley clasped in hills. The lower slopes were strewn with white villages like stars spangling a summer dusk; and beyond these, fold on fold of blue mountain, clear as gauze against the sky. The August air was lifeless, but it seemed light and vivifying after the atmosphere of the shrouded rooms through which I had been led. Their chill was on me and I hugged the sunshine.

"The duchess's apartments are beyond," said the old man.

He was the oldest man I had ever seen; so sucked back into the past that he seemed more like a memory than a living being. The one trait linking him with the actual was the fixity with which his small saurian eye held the pocket that, as I entered, had yielded a lira to the gatekeeper's child. He went on, without removing his eye:

"For two hundred years nothing has been changed in the apartments of the duchess."

"And no one lives here now?"

"No one, sir. The duke goes to Como for the summer season."

I had moved to the other end of the loggia. below me, through hanging groves, white roofs and domes flashed like a smile.

"And that's Vicenza?"

"Proprio!" The old man extended fingers as lean as the hands fading from the walls behind us. "You see the palace roof over there, just to the left of the Basilica? The one with the row of statues like birds taking flight? That's the duke's town palace, built by Palladio."

"And does the duke come there?"

"Never. In winter he goes to Rome."

"And the palace and the villa are always closed?"

"As you see—always."

"How long has this been?"

"Since I can remember."

I looked into his eyes: they were like tarnished metal mirrors reflecting nothing. "That must be a long time," I said, involuntarily.

"A long time," he assented.

I looked down on the gardens. An opulence of dahlias overran the box-borders, between cypresses that cut the sunshine like basalt shafts. Bees hung above the lavender; lizards sunned themselves on the benches and slipped through the cracks of the dry basins. Everywhere were vanishing traces of that fantastic horticulture of which our dull age has lost the art. Down the alleys maimed statues stretched their arms like rows of whining beggars; faun-eared terms grinned in the thicket, and above the laurustinus walls rose the mock ruin of a temple, falling into real ruin in the bright disintegrating air. The glare was blinding.

"Let us go in," I said.

The old man pushed open a heavy door, behind which the cold lurked like a knife.

"The duchess's apartments," he said.

Overhead and around us the same evanescent frescoes, under foot the same scagliola volutes, unrolled themselves interminably. Ebony cabinets, with colonnades of precious marbles in cunning perspective, alternated down the room with the tarnished efflorescence of gilt consoles supporting Chinese monsters; and from the chimney panel a gentleman in the Spanish habit haughtily ignored us.

"Duke Ercole II," the old man explained, "by the Genoese Priest."

It was a narrow-browed face, sallow as a wax effigy, high-nosed and cautious-lidded, as though modelled by priestly hands; the lips weak and vain rather than cruel; a quibbling mouth that would have snapped at verbal errors like a lizard catching flies, but had never learned the shape of a round yes or no. One of the duke's hands rested on the head of a dwarf, a simian creature with pearl earrings and fantastic dress; the other turned the pages of a folio propped on a skull.

"Beyond is the duchess's bedroom," the old man reminded me.

Here the shutters admitted but two narrow shafts of light, gold bars deepening the subaqueous gloom. On a dais, the bedstead, grim, nuptial, official, lifted its baldachin; a yellow Christ agonized between the curtains, and across the room a lady smiled at us from the chimney-breast.

The old man unbarred a shutter and the light touched her face. Such a face it was, with a flicker of laughter over it like the wind on a June meadow, and a singular tender pliancy of mien, as though one of Tiepolo's lenient goddesses had been busked into the stiff sheath of a seventeenth-century dress!

"No one has slept here," said the old man, "since the Duchess Violante."

"And she was—?"

"The lady there—first duchess of Duke Ercole II."

He drew a key from his pocket and unlocked a door at the farther end of the room. “The chapel,” he said. “This is the duchess’s balcony.” As I turned to follow him the duchess tossed me a side-long smile.

I stepped into a grated tribune above a chapel festooned with stucco. Pictures of bituminous saints mouldered between the pilasters; the artificial roses in the altar vases were gray with dust and age, and under the cobwebby rosettes of the vaulting a bird’s nest clung. Before the altar stood a row of tattered armchairs, and I drew back at sight of a figure kneeling near them.

“The duchess,” the old man whispered. “By the Cavaliere Bernini.”

It was the image of a woman in furred robes and spreading fraise, her hands lifted, her face addressed to the tabernacle. There was a strangeness in the sight of that immovable presence locked in prayer before an abandoned shrine. Her face was hidden, and I wondered whether it were grief or gratitude that raised her hands and drew her eyes to the altar, where no living prayer joined her marble invocation, I followed my guide down the tribune steps, impatient to see what mystic version of such terrestrial graces the ingenious artist had found—the cavaliere was master of such arts. The duchess's attitude was one of transport, as though heavenly airs fluttered her laces and the love-locks escaping from her coif. I saw how admirably the sculptor had caught the poise of her head, the tender slope of the shoulder; then I crossed over and looked into her face—it was a frozen horror. Never have hate, revolt, and agony so possessed a human countenance…

The old man crossed himself and shuffled his feet on the marble.

"The Duchess Violante," he repeated.

"The same as in the picture?"

"Eh—the same."

"But the face—what does it mean?"

He shrugged his shoulders and turned deaf eyes on me. Then he shot a glance round the sepulchral place, clutched my sleeve and said, close to my ear: "It was not always so."

"What was not?"

"The face—so terrible."

"The duchess's face?"

"The statue's. It changed after—"

"After?"

"It was put here."

"The statue's face changed—?"

He mistook my bewilderment for incredulity and his confidential finger dropped from my sleeve. "Eh, that's the story. I tell what I've heard. What do I know?" He resumed his senile shuffle across the marble. "This is a bad place to stay in—no one comes here. It's too cold. But the gentleman said, I must see everything!"

I let the lire sound. "So I must—and hear everything. This story, now—from whom did you have it?"

His hand stole back. "One that saw it, by God!"

"That saw it?"

"My grandmother, then. I'm a very old man."

"Your grandmother? Your grandmother was—?"

"The duchess's serving girl, with respect to you."

"Your grandmother? Two hundred years ago?"

"Is it too long ago? That's as God pleases. I am a very old man and she was a very old woman when I was born. When she died she was as black as a miraculous Virgin and her breath whistled like the wind in a keyhole. She told me the story when I was a little boy. She told it to me out there in the garden, on a bench by the fishpond, one summer night of the year she died. It must be true, for I can show you the very bench we sat on…"

III

NOON LAY HEAVIER on the gardens; not our live humming warmth, but the stale exhalation of dead summers. The very statues seemed to drowse like watchers by a deathbed. Lizards shot out of the cracked soil like flames and the bench in the laurustinus-niche was strewn with the blue varnished bodies of dead flies. Before us lay the fishpond, a yellow marble slab above rotting secrets. The villa looked across it, composed as a dead face, with the cypresses flanking it for candles…

IV

"…IMPOSSIBLE, YOU SAY, that my mother's mother should have been the duchess's maid? What do I know? It is so long since anything has happened here that the old things seem nearer, perhaps, than to those who live in cities . . . But how else did she know about the statue then? Answer me that, sir! That she saw with her eyes, I can swear to, and never smiled again, so she told me, till they put her first child in her arms . . . for she was taken to wife by the steward's son, Antonio, the same who had carried the letters . . . But where am I? Ah, well . . . she was a mere slip, you understand, my grandmother, when the duchess died, a niece of the upper maid, Nencia, and suffered about the duchess because of her pranks and the funny songs she knew. It's possible, you think, she may have heard from others what she afterward fancied she had seen herself? How that is, it's not for an unlettered man to say; though indeed I myself seem to have seen many of the

things she told me. This is a strange place. No one comes here, nothing changes, and the old memories stand up as distinct as the statues in the garden…

"It began the summer after they came back from the Brenta. Duke Ercole had married the lady from Venice, you must know; it was a gay city, then, I'm told, with laughter and music on the water, and the days slipped by like boats running with the tide. Well, to humor her he took her back the first autumn to the Brenta. Her father, it appears, had a grand palace there, with such gardens, bowling alleys, grottoes and casinos as never were; gondolas bobbing at the water gates, a stable full of gilt coaches, a theatre full of players, and kitchens and offices full of cooks and lackeys to serve up chocolate all day long to the fine ladies in masks and furbelows, with their pet dogs and their blackamoors and their abates. Eh!

I know it all as if I'd been there, for Nencia, you see, my grandmother's aunt, travelled with the duchess, and came back with her eyes round as platters, and not a word to say for the rest of the year to any of the lads who'd courted her here in Vicenza.

"What happened there I don't know—my grandmother could never get at the rights of it, for Nencia was mute as a fish where her lady was concerned—but when they came back to Vicenza the Duke ordered the villa set in order; and in the spring he brought the duchess here and left her. She looked happy enough, my grandmother said, and seemed no object for pity. Perhaps, after all, it was better than being shut up in Vicenza, in the tall painted rooms where priests came and went as softly as cats prowling for birds, and the duke was forever closeted in his library, talking with learned men. The duke was a scholar; you noticed he was painted with a book? Well, those that can read 'em make out that they're full of wonderful things; as a man that's been to a fair across the mountains will always tell his people at home it was beyond anything they'll ever see. As for the duchess, she was all for music, play-acting, and young company. The duke was a silent man, stepping quietly, with his eyes down, as though he'd just come from confession; when the duchess's lapdog yapped at his heels he danced like a man in a swarm of hornets; when the duchess laughed, he winced as if you'd drawn a diamond across a windowpane. And the duchess was always laughing.

"When she first came to the villa she was very busy laying out the gardens, designing grottoes, planting groves, and planning all manner of agreeable surprises in the way of water jets that drenched you unexpectedly, and hermits in caves, and wild men that jumped at you out of thickets. She had a very pretty taste in such matters, but after awhile she tired of it, and there being no one for her to talk to but her maids and the chaplain—a clumsy man deep in his books—why, she would have strolling players out from Vicenza, mountebanks and fortune-tellers from the marketplace, travelling doctors and astrologers, and all manner of trained animals. Still it could be seen that the poor lady pined for company, and her waiting women, who loved her, were glad when the Cavaliere Ascanio, the duke's cousin, came to live at the vineyard across the valley—you see the pinkish house over there in the mulberries, with a red roof and a pigeon cote?

"The Cavaliere Ascanio was a cadet of one of the great Venetian houses, pezzi grossi of the Golden Book. He had been meant for the Church, I believe, but what! he set fighting above praying and cast in his lot with the captain of the Duke of Mantua's bravi, himself a Venetian of good standing, but a little at odds with the law. Well, the next I knew, the cavaliere was in Venice again, perhaps not in good odor on account of his connection with the gentleman I speak of. Some say he tried to carry off a nun from the convent of Santa Croce; how that may be I can't say; but my grandmother declared he had enemies there, and the end of it was that on some pretext or other the Ten banished him to Vicenza. There, of course, the duke, being his kinsman, had to show him a civil face; and that was how he first came to the villa.

"He was a fine young man, beautiful as a Saint Sebastian, a rare musician, who sang his own songs to the lute in a way that used to make my grandmother's heart melt and run through her body like mulled wine. He had a good word for everybody, too, and was always dressed in the French fashion, and smelt as sweet as a bean field; and every soul about the place welcomed the sight of him.

"Well, the duchess, it seemed, welcomed it too; youth will have youth, and laughter turns to laughter; and the two matched each other like the candlesticks on an altar. The duchess—you've seen her portrait—but to hear my grandmother, sir, it no more approached her than a weed comes up to a rose. The cavaliere, indeed, as became a poet, paragoned her in his song to all the pagan goddesses of antiquity; and doubtless these were finer to look at than mere women; but so, it seemed, was she; for, to believe my grandmother, she made other women look no more than the big French fashion doll that used to be shown on Ascension days in the Piazza. She was one, at any rate, that needed no outlandish finery to beautify her; whatever dress she wore became her as feathers fit the bird; and her hair didn't get its colour by bleaching on the housetop. It glittered of itself like the threads in an Easter chasuble, and her skin was whiter than fine wheaten bread, and her mouth as sweet as a ripe fig.

"Well, sir, you could no more keep them apart than the bees and the lavender. They were always together, singing, bowling, playing cup and ball, walking in the gardens, visiting the aviaries and petting her grace's trick-dogs and monkeys. The duchess was as gay as a foal, always playing pranks and laughing, tricking out her animals like comedians, disguising herself as a peasant or a nun (you should have seen her one day pass herself off to the chaplain as a mendicant sister), or teaching the lads and girls of the vineyards to dance and sing madrigals together. The cavaliere had a singular ingenuity in planning such entertainments, and the days were hardly long enough for their diversions. But toward the end of the summer the duchess fell quiet and would hear only sad music, and the two sat much together in the gazebo at the end of the garden. It was there the duke found them one day when he drove out from Vicenza in his gilt coach. He came but once or twice a year to the villa, and it was, as my grandmother said, just a part of her poor lady's ill luck to be wearing that day the Venetian habit, which uncovered the shoulders in a way the duke always scowled at, and her curls loose and powdered with gold. Well, the three drank chocolate in the gazebo, and what happened no one knew, except that the duke, on taking leave, gave his cousin a seat in his carriage; but the cavaliere never returned.

"Winter approaching, and the poor lady thus finding herself once more alone, it was surmised among her women that she must fall into a deeper depression of spirits. But far from this being the case, she displayed such cheerfulness and equanimity of humor that my grandmother, for one, was half-vexed with her for giving no more thought to the poor young man who, all this time, was eating his heart out in the house across the valley. It is true she quitted her gold-laced gowns and wore a veil over her head; but Nencia would have it she looked the lovelier for the change, and so gave the duke greater displeasure. Certain it is that the duke drove out oftener to the villa, and though he found his lady always engaged in some innocent pursuit, such as embroidery or music, or playing games with her young women, yet he always went away with a sour look and a whispered word to the chaplain. Now as to the chaplain, my grandmother owned there had been a time when her grace had not handled him over-wisely. For, according to Nencia, it seems that his reverence, who seldom approached the duchess, being buried in his library like a mouse in a cheese—well, one day he made bold to appeal to her for a sum of money, a large sum, Nencia said, to buy certain tall books, a chest full of them, that a foreign peddler had brought him; whereupon the duchess, who could never abide a book, breaks out at him with a laugh and a flash of her old spirit—'Holy Mother of God, must I have more books about me? I was nearly smothered with them in the first year of my marriage;' and the chaplain turning red at the affront, she added: 'You may buy them and welcome, my good chaplain, if you can find the money; but as for me, I am yet seeking a way to pay for my turquoise necklace, and the statue of Daphne at the end of the bowling green, and the Indian parrot that my black boy brought me last Michaelmas from the Bohemians—so you see I've no money to waste on trifles;' and as he backs out awkwardly she tosses at him, over her shoulder: 'You should pray to Saint Blandina to open the duke's pocket!' to which he returned, very quietly, 'Your excellency's suggestion is an admirable one, and I have already entreated that blessed martyr to open the duke's understanding.'

"Thereat, Nencia said (who was standing by), the duchess flushed wonderfully red and waved him out of the room; and then 'Quick!' she cried to my grandmother (who was too glad to run on such errands), 'Call me Antonio, the gardener's boy, to the box-garden; I've a word to say to him about the new clove-carnations…

"Now, I may not have told you, sir, that in the crypt under the chapel there has stood, for more generations than a man can count, a stone coffin containing a thigh bone of the blessed Saint Blandina of Lyons, a relic offered, I've been told, by some great duke of France to one of our own dukes when they fought the Turk together; and the object, ever since, of particular veneration in this illustrious family. Now, since the duchess had been left to herself, it was observed she affected a fervent devotion to this relic, praying often in the chapel and even causing the stone slab that covered the entrance to the crypt to be replaced by a wooden one, that she might at will descend and kneel by the coffin. This was matter of edification to all the household, and should have been peculiarly pleasing to the chaplain; but, with respect to you, he was the kind of man who brings a sour mouth to the eating of the sweetest apple.

"However that may be, the duchess, when she dismissed him, was seen running

to the garden, where she talked earnestly with the boy Antonio about the new clove-carnations; and the rest of the day she sat indoors and played sweetly on the virginal. Now Nencia always had it in mind that her grace had made a mistake in refusing that request of the chaplain's; but she said nothing, for to talk reason to the duchess was of no more use than praying for rain in a drought.

"Winter came early that year, there was snow on the hills by All Souls, the wind stripped the gardens, and the lemon trees were nipped in the lemon house. The duchess kept her room in this black season, sitting over the fire, embroidering, reading books of devotion (which was a thing she had never done), and praying frequently in the chapel. As for the chaplain, it was a place he never set foot in but to say mass in the morning, with the duchess overhead in the tribune, and the servants aching with rheumatism on the marble floor. The chaplain himself hated the cold, and galloped through the mass like a man with witches after him. The rest of the day he spent in his library, over a brazier, with his eternal books...

"You'll wonder, sir, if I'm ever to get to the gist of the story; and I've gone slowly, I own, for fear of what's coming. Well, the winter was long and hard. When it fell cold the duke ceased to come out from Vicenza, and not a soul had the duchess to speak to but her maidservants and the gardeners about the place. Yet it was wonderful, my grandmother said, how she kept her brave colours and her spirits; only it was remarked that she prayed longer in the chapel, where a brazier was kept burning for her all day. When the young are denied their natural pleasures, they turn often enough to religion; and it was a mercy, as my grandmother said, that she, who had scarce a live sinner to speak to, should take such comfort in a dead saint.

"My grandmother seldom saw her that winter, for though she showed a brave front to all, she kept more and more to herself, choosing to have only Nencia about her, and dismissing even her when she went to pray. For her devotion had that mark of true piety, that she wished it not to be observed; so that Nencia had strict orders, on the chaplain's approach, to warn her mistress if she happened to be in prayer.

"Well, the winter passed, and spring was well forward, when my grandmother one evening had a bad fright. That it was her own fault I won't deny, for she'd been down the lime-walk with Antonio when her aunt fancied her to be stitching in her chamber; and seeing a sudden light in Nencia's window, she took fright lest her disobedience be found out. and ran up quickly through the laurel grove to the house. Her way lay by the chapel, and as she crept past it, meaning to slip in through the scullery, and groping her way, for the dark had fallen and the moon was scarce up, she heard a crash close behind her, as though someone had dropped from a window of the chapel. The young fool's heart turned over, but she looked round as she ran, and there, sure enough, was a man scuttling across the terrace; and as he doubled the corner of the house my grandmother swore she caught the whisk of the chaplain's skirts. Now that was a strange thing, certainly; for why should the chaplain be getting out of the chapel window when he might have passed through the door? For you may have noticed, sir, there's a door leads from the chapel into the saloon on the ground floor; the only other way out being through the duchess's tribune.

"Well, my grandmother turned the matter over, and next time she met Antonio in the lime-walk (which, by reason of her fright, was not for some days) she laid before him what had happened; but to her surprise he only laughed, and said, 'You little simpleton, he wasn't getting out of the window, he was trying to look in;' and not another word could she get from him.

"So the season moved on to Easter, and news came the duke had gone to Rome for that holy festivity. His comings and goings made no change at the villa, and yet there was no one there but felt easier to think his yellow face was on the far side of the Apennines, unless, perhaps, it was the chaplain.

"Well, it was one day in May that the duchess, who had walked long with Nencia on the terrace, rejoicing at the sweetness of the prospect and the pleasant scent of the gilly-flowers in the stone vases, the duchess toward midday withdrew to her rooms, giving orders that her dinner should be served in her bedchamber. My grandmother helped to carry in the dishes, and observed, she said, the singular beauty of the duchess, who, in honor of the fine weather, had put on a gown of shot-silver and hung her bare shoulders with pearls, so that she looked fit to dance at court with an emperor. She had ordered, too, a rare repast for a lady that heeded so little what she ate—jellies, game pastries, fruits in syrup, spiced cakes, and a flagon of Greek wine; and she nodded and clapped her hands as the women set it before her, saying, again and again, 'I shall eat well today.'

"But presently another mood seized her; she turned from the table, called for her rosary, and said to Nencia: 'The fine weather has made me neglect my devotions. I must say a litany before I dine.'

"She ordered the women out and barred the door, as her custom was; and Nencia and my grandmother went downstairs to work in the linen-room.

"Now the linen room gives on the courtyard, and suddenly my grandmother saw a strange sight approaching. First up the avenue came the duke's carriage (whom all thought to be in Rome), and after it, drawn by a long string of mules and oxen, a cart carrying what looked like a kneeling figure wrapped in death clothes. The strangeness of it struck the girl dumb and the duke's coach was at the door before she had the wit to cry out that it was coming. Nencia, when she saw it, went white and ran out of the room. My grandmother followed, scared by her face, and the two fled along the corridor to the chapel. On the way they met the chaplain, deep in a book, who asked in surprise where they were running, and when they said, to announce the duke's arrival, he fell into such astonishment, and asked them so many questions and uttered such ohs and ahs that by the time he let them by the duke was at their heels. Nencia reached the chapel door first and cried out that the duke was coming; and before she had a reply he was at her side, with the chaplain following.

"A moment later the door opened and there stood the duchess. She held her rosary in one hand and had drawn a scarf over her shoulders; but they shone through it like the moon in a mist, and her countenance sparkled with beauty.

"The duke took her hand with a bow. 'Madam,' he said, 'I could have had no greater happiness than thus to surprise you at your devotions.'

"'My own happiness,' she replied, 'would have been greater had your excellency prolonged it by giving me notice of your arrival.'

"'Had you expected me, Madam,' said he, 'your appearance could scarcely have been more fitted to the occasion. Few ladies of your youth and beauty array themselves to venerate a saint as they would to welcome a lover.'

"'Sir,' she answered, 'having never enjoyed the latter opportunity, I am constrained to make the most of the former.—What's that?' she cried, falling back, and the rosary dropped from her hand.

"There was a loud noise at the other end of the saloon, as of a heavy object being dragged down the passage; and presently a dozen men were seen haling across the threshold the shrouded thing from the ox-cart. The duke waved his hand toward it. 'That,' said he, 'Madam, is a tribute to your extraordinary piety. I have heard with peculiar satisfaction of your devotion to the blessed relics in this chapel, and to commemorate a zeal which neither the rigors of winter nor the sultriness of summer could abate, I have ordered a sculptured image of you, marvellously executed by the Cavaliere Bernini, to be placed before the altar over the entrance to the crypt.'

"The duchess, who had grown pale, nevertheless smiled playfully at this. 'As to commemorating my piety,' she said. 'I recognize there one of your excellency's pleasantries—'

"'A pleasantry?' the duke interrupted; and he made a sign to the men, who had now reached the threshold of the chapel. In an instant the wrappings fell from the figure, and there knelt the duchess to the life. A cry of wonder rose from all, but the duchess herself stood whiter than the marble.

"'You will see,' says the duke, 'this is no pleasantry, but a triumph of the incomparable Bernini's chisel. The likeness was done from your miniature portrait by the divine Elisabetta Sirani, which I sent to the master some six months ago, with what results all must admire.'

"'Six months!' cried the duchess, and seemed about to fall; but his excellency caught her by the hand.

"'Nothing,' he said, 'could better please me than the excessive emotion you display, for true piety is ever modest, and your thanks could not take a form that better became you. And now,' says he to the men, 'let the image be put in place.'

"By this, life seemed to have returned to the duchess, and she answered him with a deep reverence. 'That I should be overcome by so unexpected a grace, your excellency admits to be natural; but what honors you accord it is my privilege to accept, and I entreat only that in mercy to my modesty the image be placed in the remotest part of the chapel.'

"At that the duke darkened. 'What! You would have this masterpiece of a renowned chisel, which, I disguise not, cost me the price of a good vineyard in gold pieces, you would have it thrust out of sight like the work of a village stonecutter?'

"'It is my semblance, not the sculptor's work, I desire to conceal'

"'If you are fit for my house, Madam, you are fit for God's, and entitled to the place of honor in both. Bring the statue forward, you dawdlers!' he called out to the men.

"The duchess fell back submissively. 'You are right, sir, as always; but I would at least have the image stand on the left of the altar, that, looking up, it may behold your excellency's seat in the tribune.'

"'A pretty thought, Madam, for which I thank you; but I design before long to put my companion image on the other side of the altar; and the wife's place, as you know, is at her husband's right hand.'

"'True, my lord—but, again, if my poor

presentment is to have the unmerited honor of kneeling beside yours, why not place both before the altar, where it is our habit to pray in life?'

"'And where, Madam, should we kneel if they took our places? Besides,' says the duke, still speaking very blandly, 'I have a more particular purpose in placing your image over the entrance to the crypt; for not only would I thereby mark your special devotion to the blessed saint who rests there, but, by sealing up the opening in the pavement, would assure the perpetual preservation of that holy martyr's bones, which hitherto have been too thoughtlessly exposed to sacrilegious attempts.'

"'What attempts, my lord?' cries the duchess. 'No one enters this chapel without my leave.'

"'So I have understood, and can well believe from what I have learned of your piety; yet at night a malefactor might break in through a window, Madam, and your excellency not know it.'

"'I'm a light sleeper,' said the duchess.

"The duke looked at her gravely. 'Indeed?' said he. 'A bad sign at your age. I must see that you are provided with a sleeping draught.'

"The duchess's eyes filled. 'You would deprive me, then, of the consolation of visiting those venerable relics?'

"'I would have you keep eternal guard over them, knowing no one to whose care they may more fittingly be entrusted.'

"By this the image was brought close to the wooden slab that covered the entrance to the crypt, when the duchess, springing forward, placed herself in the way.

"'Sir, let the statue be put in place tomorrow, and suffer me, tonight, to say a last prayer beside those holy bones.'

"The duke stepped instantly to her side.

'Well thought, Madam; I will go down with you now, and we will pray together.'

"'Sir, your long absences have, alas! given me the habit of solitary devotion, and I confess that any presence is distracting.'

"'Madam, I accept your rebuke. Hitherto, it is true, the duties of my station have constrained me to long absences; but henceforward I remain with you while you live. Shall we go down into the crypt together?'

"'No; for I fear for your excellency's ague. The air there is excessively damp.'

"'The more reason you should no longer be exposed to it; and to prevent the intemperance of your zeal I will at once make the place inaccessible.'

"The duchess at this fell on her knees on the slab, weeping excessively and lifting her hands to heaven.

"'Oh,' she cried, 'you are cruel, sir, to deprive me of access to the sacred relics that have enabled me to support with resignation the solitude to which your excellency's duties have condemned me; and if prayer and meditation give me any authority to pronounce on such matters, suffer me to warn you, sir, that I fear the blessed Saint Blandina will punish us for thus abandoning her venerable remains!'

"The duke at this seemed to pause, for he was a pious man, and my grandmother thought she saw him exchange a glance with the chaplain; who, stepping timidly forward, with his eyes on the ground, said, 'There is, indeed, much wisdom in her excellency's words, but I would suggest, sir, that her pious wish might be met, and the saint more conspicuously honored, by transferring the relics from the crypt to a place beneath the altar.'

"'True!' cried the duke, 'and it shall be done at once.'

"But thereat the duchess rose to her feet with a terrible look.

"'No,' she cried, 'by the body of God! For it shall not be said that, after your excellency has chosen to deny every request I addressed to him, I owe his consent to the solicitation of another!'

"The chaplain turned red and the duke yellow, and for a moment neither spoke.

"Then the duke said, 'Here are words enough, Madam. Do you wish the relics brought up from the crypt?'

"'I wish nothing that I owe to another's intervention!'

"'Put the image in place then,' says the duke, furiously; and handed her grace to a chair.

"She sat there, my grandmother said, straight as an arrow, her hands locked, her head high, her eyes on the duke, while the statue was dragged to its place; then she stood up and turned away. As she passed by Nencia, 'Call me Antonio,' she whispered; but before the words were out of her mouth the duke stepped between them.

"'Madam,' says he, all smiles now, 'I have travelled straight from Rome to bring you the sooner this proof of my esteem. I lay last night at Monselice and have been on the road since daybreak. Will you not invite me to sup?'

"'Surely, my lord,' said the duchess. 'It shall be laid in the dining parlor within the hour.'

"'Why not in your chamber and at once. Madam? Since I believe it is your custom to sup there.'

"'In my chamber?' says the duchess, in disorder.

"'Have you anything against it?' he asked.

"'Assuredly not, sir. if you will give me time to prepare myself.'

"'I will wait in your cabinet,' said the duke.

"At that, said my grandmother, the duchess gave one look, as the souls in hell may have looked when the gates closed on our Lord; then she called Nencia and passed to her chamber.

"What happened there my grandmother could never learn, but that the duchess, in great haste, dressed herself with extraordinary splendor, powdering her hair with gold, painting her face and bosom, and covering herself with jewels till she shone like our Lady of Loreto; and hardly were these preparations complete when the duke entered from the cabinet, followed by the servants, carrying supper. Thereupon the duchess dismissed Nencia, and what follows my grandmother learned from a pantry lad who brought up the dishes and waited in the cabinet; for only the duke's bodyservant entered the bedchamber.

"Well, according to this boy, sir, who was looking and listening with his whole body, as it were, because he had never before been suffered so near the duchess, it appears that the noble couple sat down in great good humor, the duchess playfully reproving her husband for his long absence, while the duke swore that to look so beautiful was the best way of punishing him. In this tone the talk continued, with such gay sallies on the part of the duchess, such tender advances on the duke's, that the lad declared they were for all the world like a pair of lovers courting on a summer's night in the vineyard; and so it went till the servant brought in the mulled wine.

"'Ah,' the duke was saying at that moment, 'this agreeable evening repays me for the many dull ones I have spent away from you; nor do I remember to have enjoyed such laughter since the afternoon last year when we drank chocolate in the gazebo with my cousin Ascanio. And that reminds me,' he said, 'is my cousin in good health?'

"'I have no reports of it,' says the duchess. 'But your excellency should taste these figs stewed in malmsey——'

"'I am in the mood to taste whatever you offer,' said he; and as she helped him to the figs he added, 'If my enjoyment were not complete as it is, I could almost wish my cousin Ascanio were with us. The fellow is rare good company at supper. What do you say, Madam? I hear he's still in the country; shall we send for him to join us?'

"'Ah,' said the duchess, with a sigh and a languishing look, 'I see your excellency wearies of me already.'

"'I, Madam? Ascanio is a capital good fellow, but to my mind his chief merit at this moment is his absence. It inclines me so tenderly to him, that, by God, I could empty a glass to his good health.'

"With that the duke caught up his goblet and signed to the servant to fill the duchess's.

"'Here's to the cousin,' he cried, standing, 'who has the good taste to stay away when he's not wanted. I drink to his very long life—and you, Madam?'

"At this the duchess, who had sat staring at him with a changed face, rose also and lifted her glass to her lips.

"'And I to his happy death,' says she in a wild voice; and as she spoke the empty goblet dropped from her hand and she fell face down on the floor.

"The duke shouted to her women that she had swooned, and they came and lifted her to the bed... She suffered horribly all night, Nencia said, twisting herself like a heretic at the stake, but without a word escaping her. The duke watched by her, and toward daylight sent for the chaplain; but by this she was unconscious and, her teeth being locked, our Lord's body could not be passed through them.

"THE DUKE ANNOUNCED to his relations that his lady had died after partaking too freely of spiced wine and an omelet of carp's roe, at a supper she had prepared in honour of his return; and the next year he brought home a new duchess, who gave him a son and five daughters..."

V

THE SKY HAD turned to a steel gray, against which the villa stood out sallow and inscrutable. A wind strayed there a yellow leaf from the sycamores; and the hills across the valley were purple as thunderclouds.

"AND THE STATUE—?" I asked.

"Ah, the statue. Well, sir, this is what my grandmother told me, here on this very bench where we're sitting. The poor child, who worshipped the duchess as a girl of her years will worship a beautiful kind mistress, spent a night of horror, you may fancy, shut out from her lady's room, hearing the cries that came from it, and seeing, as she crouched in her corner, the women rush to and fro with wild looks, the duke's lean face in the door, and the chaplain skulking in the antechamber with his eyes on his breviary. No one minded her that night or the next morning; and toward dusk, when it became known the duchess was no more, the poor girl felt the pious wish to say a prayer for her dead mistress. She crept to the chapel and stole in unobserved. The place was empty and dim, but as she advanced she heard a low moaning, and coming in front of the statue she saw that its face, the day before so sweet and smiling, had the look on it that you know—and the moaning seemed to come from its lips. My grandmother turned cold, but something, she said afterward, kept her from calling or shrieking out, and she turned and ran from the place. In the passage she fell in a swoon; and when she came to her senses, in her own chamber, she heard that the duke had locked the chapel door and forbidden any to set foot there...

The place was never opened again till the duke died, some ten years later; and then it was that the other servants, going in with the new heir, saw for the first time the horror that my grandmother had kept in her bosom.

"And the crypt?" I asked. "Has it never been opened?"

"Heaven forbid, sir!" cried the old man, crossing himself. "Was it not the duchess's express wish that the relics should not be disturbed?"

EDITH WHARTON (1862–1937) was an American novelist and short story writer known for her sharp portrayals of upper-class New York society. She became the first woman to win the Pulitzer Prize for Fiction for her novel *The Age of Innocence* (1921).

SETH'S COMICS AND drawings have appeared in the *New York Times*, the *New Yorker*, the *Globe and Mail*, and countless other publications.

His graphic novel *Clyde Fans* won the prestigious Festival d'Angoulême's Prix Spécial du Jury.

He lives in Guelph, Ontario, with his wife, Tania, in an old house he has named "Inkwell's End."

Publisher's Note: "The Duchess at Prayer" was first published
in *Scribner's Magazine*, Vol. 13, August 1900

Library and Archives Canada Cataloguing in Publication

Title: The duchess at prayer / Edith Wharton ; a ghost story
for Christmas, designed & decorated by Seth.
Names: Wharton, Edith, 1862–1937, author. | Seth, 1962–
illustrator.
Description: Series statement: Seth's Christmas ghost stories
Identifiers: Canadiana 20260201200
ISBN 9781771967440 (softcover)
Subjects: LCGFT: Ghost stories. | LCGFT: Christmas fiction.
LCGFT: Short stories.
Classification: LCC PS3545.H16 D83 2026 | DDC 813/.52—dc23

Readied for the press by Daniel Wells
Illustrated and designed by Seth
Copyedited by Ashley Van Elswyk
Typeset by Ingrid Paulson

PRINTED AND BOUND IN CANADA